D1604502

PICNIC
PANDEMONIUM

For a free color catalog describing Gareth Stevens' list of high-quality children's books, call 1-800-341-3569 (USA) or 1-800-461-9120 (Canada).

For my father
M.C.B.

Library of Congress Cataloging-in-Publication Data

Butler, M. Christina.
    Picnic pandemonium / Story by M. Christina Butler ; illustrated by Meg Rutherford.
        p. cm.
    Summary: Several jungle animals try to carry a picnic basket to the river with humorous results.
    ISBN 0-8368-0433-3
    [1. Jungle animals—Fiction. 2. Picnicking—Fiction.] I. Rutherford, Meg, ill.
  II. Title.
  PZ7.B97738Pi   1990
  [E]—dc20   90-10148

North American edition first published in 1991 by
Gareth Stevens Children's Books
1555 North RiverCenter Drive, Suite 201
Milwaukee, Wisconsin 53212, USA

This format copyright © 1991 by Gareth Stevens, Inc.
Text copyright © 1989 by M. Christina Butler
Illustrations copyright © 1989 by Meg Rutherford
First published as *Where Are My Bananas?* in Great Britain in 1989
by Macdonald Children's Books, Simon & Schuster International Group

Cover design: Kate Kriege

Printed in the United States of America

1 2 3 4 5 6 7 8 9 97 96 95 94 93 92 91

PICNIC
PANDEMONIUM

M. CHRISTINA BUTLER   MEG RUTHERFORD

Gareth Stevens Children's Books
MILWAUKEE

GOLD STAR FIRST READERS

Picnic Pandemonium by M. Christina Butler
Help! by Nigel Croser and Rhoda Irene Sherwood

By Lynley Dodd:

The Apple Tree
A Dragon in a Wagon
Hairy Maclary from Donaldson's Dairy
Hairy Maclary Scattercat
Hairy Maclary's Bone
Hairy Maclary's Caterwaul Caper
Hairy Maclary's Rumpus at the Vet
The Smallest Turtle
Wake Up, Bear

The hot, bright sun shone
down on the jungle.

"What should we do
today?" asked Monkey.

"It's too hot for housework," sighed Elephant.

"It's too hot to gather honey," rumbled Bear.

6

"It's too hot to tease tigers," cried Monkey.

"It's too hot to chase monkeys," growled Tiger.

7

"It's not too hot for a picnic!"
piped up Mouse.

"A picnic!" cried Monkey.
"Let's do it!"

"In the shade!" sighed
Elephant.

"By the river!"
rumbled Bear.
"And with all our
favorite food!"
growled Tiger.

9

Everyone had a job to do.
Mouse brought a chunk of cheese.
Monkey brought a bunch of bananas.
Tiger brought a bag of potato chips.
Bear brought a pot full of honey.
And Elephant brought some apples
and a basket.

It was Elephant's job to pack the basket. It was Bear's job to carry it.

And so, off they went . . .

to the river.

They hadn't gone far when
Bear stopped to make
sure his honey was
safe. It was
nowhere
to be found.

"Who stole my
honey?"
he growled.

14

"Not I!" purred Tiger.
"Not I!" giggled Monkey.
"Not I!" squeaked Mouse.

"Hold it!" trumpeted Elephant.
"*I* must have left it behind.
So *I'll* go back and get it."

Elephant came back with
the honey. Now Bear
packed the basket.
And Elephant carried it.

And so, off they went again.

They hadn't gone far when Elephant began to feel hungry. He reached in the basket for his apples. They were nowhere to be found.

"Who stole my apples?" he trumpeted.

"Not I!" squealed Mouse.
"Not I!" roared Tiger.
"Not I!" yowled Monkey.

19

"Hold it!" growled Bear.
"*I* must have left them in
the grass. So *I'll* go back
and get them."

Bear came back with the apples.
Tiger began to pack the basket.

"This time, *I'll* hold on to the food,"
said Monkey.

With that, he grabbed the basket
and swung into the treetops.

Stamping his feet, Elephant said, "That's the last we'll see of him." "And our picnic," growled Bear. "Maybe and maybe not," purred Tiger. "Let's go on to the river."

So on they went as Monkey watched from high in the trees.

It wasn't long before Monkey reached into the basket for his bananas. They were nowhere to be found.

"Who stole my bananas?"

Monkey couldn't find his bananas,
so he tossed the basket away.
Everything came tumbling down.

24

The rest of the animals
scrambled madly about.
"My apples!" thundered
Elephant, as they banged
him on the head.
"My honey!" howled Bear.
"My chips!"
bellowed Tiger.
"My cheese!"
squealed Mouse.

Monkey jabbered from the
trees above:
"Where are my bananas?
Where are my bananas?
Where are my bananas?"

"Quiet!" roared Tiger.
"*I've* got your bananas.

"You grabbed the basket before I could put them in. Now, we'll *all* pack the food. And *I'll* carry the basket."

"And *I'll* ride inside," squeaked Mouse, "just to make sure nothing falls out."

So off they went again.

At last they reached the river.
What fun they had diving and
splashing in the cool water!

"Hold it!" snarled Tiger.
"Has anyone seen Mouse?"

28

"Not I!" grinned Monkey.
"Not I!" gurgled Bear.
"Not I!" snorted Elephant.

So where was Mouse?

Mouse?
Mouse was still in the basket. And what about the food? Well, as
you can see, the food was still in the basket, too . . . you might say!